Owl in a towel

Lesley Sims

Illustrated by David Semple

D0231459

90710 000 503 569

Look!
Who can fly high in the sky,
then swoop down to the ground?

It's SuperOwl! (Her cape's towel.)

She hears a growl... and then a howl.

A villain's on the run.

A quick rest, then she's off again.
It's stormy out at sea.

A ship is stuck on sharp, dark rocks
and she must set it free.

Now she must race to outer space,
to save a speeding rocket.

A massive comet's in its path
and SuperOwl must block it.

She soars around the world all night.
She answers every call.

"Where are you, Owl?" a voice rings out. "It's time for bath and bed."

"Your cape is just a towel," says Dad, "and you are just an owl.

No more games. We're going home.
And don't give me that scowl."

Baby Toad is in the road.
He's sitting there in shock.

In a flash, Owl's swooping down.

"Be careful!" cries her dad.

"Well done!" says Dad. "I'm proud of you. But that's a tattered cape."

Let's make a towel for SuperOwl.

About phonics

Phonics is a method of teaching reading which is used extensively in today's schools. At its heart is an emphasis on identifying the *sounds* of letters, or combinations of letters, that are then put together to make words. These sounds are known as phonemes.

Starting to read

Learning to read is an important milestone for any child. The process can begin well before children start to learn letters and put them together to read words. The sooner children can discover books and enjoy stories and language, the better they will be prepared for reading themselves, first with the help of an adult and then independently.

You can find out more about phonics on the Usborne website at **usborne.com/Phonics**

Phonemic awareness

An important early stage in pre-reading and early reading is developing phonemic awareness: that is, listening out for the sounds within words. Rhymes, rhyming stories and alliteration are excellent ways of encouraging phonemic awareness.

In this story, your child will soon identify the *ow* sound, as in **owl** and **towel.** Look out, too, for rhymes such as **sea** – **free** and **race** – **space.**

Hearing your child read

If your child is reading a story to you, don't rush to correct mistakes, but be ready to prompt or guide if he or she is struggling. Above all, do give plenty of praise and encouragement.

Edited by Jenny Tyler
Designed by Hope Reynolds

Reading consultants: Alison Kelly and Anne Washtell
With thanks to Harry Whibley (age 4)

First published in 2022 by Usborne Publishing Ltd., Usborne House, 83-85 Saffron Hill,
London EC1N 8RT, England. usborne.com Copyright © 2022 Usborne Publishing Ltd. The name
Usborne and the Balloon logo are Trade Marks of Usborne Publishing Ltd. All rights reserved.
No part of this publication may be reproduced, stored in a retrieval system or transmitted
in any form or by any means without the prior permission of the publisher. UE.